10.00 **DATE DUE**

NOV 1 9 2007	
JUL 2 6 2010	
AUG 1 0 2010	
JUL 2 6 2011	
JUN 1 2 2014	

The Cat Who Barked

El gato que ladró

Learn to Read Series
Book 18

Cataloging-in-Publication Data

Sargent, Dave, 1941–
    The cat who barked = El gato que ladró /
by Dave and Pat Sargent ; illustrated by
Laura Robinson.—Prairie Grove, AR :
Ozark Publishing, c2004.
    p. cm. (Learn to read series ; 18)

    Bilingual.
    Cover Title.
    SUMMARY: A little cat thinks it's a
dog because it barks like a dog and scratches
fleas.
    ISBN 1-56763-995-X (hc)
        1-56763-996-8 (pbk)

    [1. Animals—Fiction.] I. Sargent, Pat,
1936– II. Robinson, Laura, 1973– ill. III.
Title. IV. Series.
    PZ7.S2465Ic 2004
    [E]—dc21   00-012635

Printed in the United States of America

The Cat Who Barked
El gato que ladró

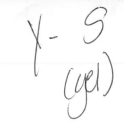

Learn to Read Series
Book 18

by Dave and Pat Sargent

Illustrated by Laura Robinson

Ozark Publishing, Inc.
P.O. Box 228
Prairie Grove, AR 72753

Dave and Pat Sargent, authors of the extremely popular Animal Pride Series, plus many other books, visit schools all over the United States, free of charge.

If you would like to have Dave and Pat visit your school, please ask your librarian to call 1-800-321-5671.

The Cat Who Barked
El gato que ladró

Learn to Read Series
Book 18

I am a cat. I am a big cat.

Yo soy un gato. Yo soy un gato grande.

Do cats bark? I do! "Bow wow!"

¿Ladran los gatos? ¡Yo sí! <<¡Guau Guau!>>

I am a cat, but I like to bark.

Yo soy un gato pero me gusta ladrar.

I like to bark loud. I like to bark very loud.

Me gusta ladrar fuerte. Me gusta ladrar muy fuerte.

I chase dogs. I chase big dogs.

Yo cazo perros. Yo cazo perros grandes.

I eat bones. I can even climb trees.

Yo como huesos. Hasta yo trepo los árboles.

I have one head. I have one mouth.

Yo tengo una cabeza. Yo tengo una boca.

I have two eyes. I have two ears.

Yo tengo dos ojos. Yo tengo dos orejas.

I have four legs. I have a neck.

Yo tengo cuatro patas. Yo tengo un cuello.

I have one tail, and my tail wags.

Yo tengo una cola, y meneo mi cola.

I bark like a dog. I go, "Bow wow!"

Yo ladro como un perro. Yo digo: <<¡Guau Guau!>>

Do I look like a dog? Don't ask me!

¿Me parezco a un perro? ¡Yo qué sé!

Do I smell like a dog? I really don't know.

¿Huelo como un perro? En realidad no lo sé.

I sit. I roll over. I can even play dead.

Yo me siento. Yo me revuelco. Hasta puedo hacerme el muerto.

Am I a dog? I think I am.

¿Soy yo un perro? Pienso que sí.

I do what dogs do. I go, "Bow wow!"

Yo hago lo que perros hacen. Yo digo: <<¡Guau Guau!>>

I scratch my fleas. I dig in the ground.

Yo me rasco mis pulgas. Yo cavo en la tierra.

I bark like a dog, so...I am a dog!

Yo ladro como un perro, por eso, ¡yo soy un perro!